DE AMICITIA
and
THE PUNCTILIOUSNESS
OF DON SEBASTIAN

DE AMICITIA
and
THE PUNCTILIOUSNESS OF DON SEBASTIAN

W. Somerset Maugham

𝒫𝒫
Portmay Press
New York

These works by William Somerset Maugham were originally published in 1899 in *Orientations*, published by T. Fisher Unwin, London, and are now part of the public domain.

Cover image courtesy of The Metropolitan Museum's Open Access initiative: Vincent Van Gogh, *The Flowering Orchard* (1888), The Mr. and Mrs. Henry Ittleson Jr. Purchase Fund, 1956.

Published in 2020 by Portmay Press, New York

ISBN 978-1-7360536-1-4 (paperback)
ISBN 979-8-9860337-3-0 (ebook)

Project management and design by Emily Albarillo

PP
Portmay Press
244 Madison Avenue
New York, NY 10016
www.portmaypress.com

Contents

DE AMICITIA

I

They were walking home from the theatre.

'Well, Mr White,' said Valentia, 'I think it was just fine.'

'It was magnificent!' replied Mr White.

And they were separated for a moment by the crowd, streaming up from the Français towards the Opera and the Boulevards.

'I think, if you don't mind,' she said, 'I'll take your arm, so that we shouldn't get lost.'

He gave her his arm, and they walked through the Louvre and over the river on their way to the Latin Quarter.

Valentia was an art student and Ferdinand White was a poet. Ferdinand considered Valentia the only woman who had ever been able to paint, and Valentia told Ferdinand that he was the only man she had met who knew anything about Art without being himself an artist. On her arrival in Paris, a year before, she had immediately inscribed herself, at the offices of the *New York Herald*, Valentia Stewart, Cincinnati, Ohio, U.S.A. She settled down in a respectable pension, and within a week was painting vigorously. Ferdinand White arrived from Oxford at about the same time, hired a dirty room in a shabby hotel, ate his meals at cheap restaurants in the Boulevard St Michel, read Stephen Mallarmé, and flattered himself that he was leading '*la vie de Bohême.*'

After two months, the Fates brought the pair together, and Ferdinand began to take his meals at Valentia's *pension*. They went to the museums together; and in the Sculpture Gallery at the Louvre, Ferdinand would discourse on ancient Greece in general and on Plato in particular, while among the pictures Valentia would lecture on tones and values and chiaroscuro. Ferdinand renounced Ruskin and all his works; Valentia read the Symposium. Frequently in the evening they went to the theatre; sometimes to the Français, but more often to the Odéon; and after the performance they would discuss the play, its art, its technique—above all, its ethics. Ferdinand explained the piece he had in contemplation, and Valentia talked of the picture she meant to paint for next year's Salon; and the lady told her friends that her companion was the cleverest man she had met in her life, while he told his that she was the only really sympathetic and intelligent girl he had ever known. Thus were united in bonds of amity, Great Britain on the one side and the United States of America and Ireland on the other.

But when Ferdinand spoke of Valentia to the few Frenchmen he knew, they asked him,—

'But this Miss Stewart—is she pretty?'

'Certainly—in her American way; a long face, with the hair parted in the middle and hanging over the nape of the neck. Her mouth is quite classic.'

'And have you never kissed the classic mouth?'

'I? Never!'

'Has she a good figure?'

'Admirable!'

'And yet—Oh, you English!' And they smiled and shrugged their shoulders as they said, 'How English!'

'But, my good fellow,' cried Ferdinand, in execrable French, 'you don't understand. We are friends, the best of friends.'

They shrugged their shoulders more despairingly than ever.

II

They stood on the bridge and looked at the water and the dark masses of the houses on the Latin side, with the twin towers of Notre Dame rising dimly behind them. Ferdinand thought of the Thames at night, with the barges gliding slowly down, and the twinkling of the lights along the Embankment.

'It must be a little like that in Holland,' she said, 'but without the lights and with greater stillness.'

'When do you start?'

She had been making preparations for spending the summer in a little village near Amsterdam, to paint.

'I can't go now,' cried Valentia. 'Corrie Sayles is going home, and there's no one else I can go with. And I can't go alone. Where are you going?'

'I? I have no plans. . . . I never make plans.'

They paused, looking at the reflections in the water. Then she said,—

'I don't see why you shouldn't come to Holland with me!'

He did not know what to think; he knew she had been reading the Symposium.

'After all,' she said, 'there's no reason why one shouldn't go away with a man as well as with a woman.'

His French friends would have suggested that there were many reasons why one should go away with a woman rather than a man; but, like his companion, Ferdinand looked at it in the light of pure friendship.

'When one comes to think of it, I really don't see why we shouldn't. And the mere fact of staying at the same hotel can make no difference to either of us. We shall both have our work—you your painting, and I my play.'

As they considered it, the idea was distinctly pleasing; they wondered that it had not occurred to them before. Sauntering homewards, they discussed the details, and in half an hour had decided on the plan of their journey, the date and the train.

Next day Valentia went to say good-bye to the old French painter whom all the American girls called Popper. She found him in a capacious dressing-gown, smoking cigarettes.

'Well, my dear,' he said, 'what news?'

'I'm going to Holland to paint windmills.'

'A very laudable ambition. With your mother?'

'My good Popper, my mother's in Cincinnati. I'm going with Mr White.'

'With Mr White?' He raised his eyebrows. 'You are very frank about it.'

'Why—what do you mean?'

He put on his glasses and looked at her carefully.

'Does it not seem to you a rather—curious thing for a young girl of your age to go away with a young man of the age of Mr Ferdinand White?'

'Good gracious me! One would think I was doing something that had never been done before!'

'Oh, many a young man has gone travelling with a young woman, but they generally start by a night train, and arrive at the station in different cabs.'

'But surely, Popper, you don't mean to insinuate—Mr White and I are going to Holland as friends.'

'Friends!'

He looked at her more curiously than ever.

'One can have a man friend as well as a girl friend,' she continued. 'And I don't see why he shouldn't be just as good a friend.'

'The danger is that he become too good.'

'You misunderstand me entirely, Popper; we are friends, and nothing but friends.'

'You are entirely off your head, my child.'

'Ah! you're a Frenchman, you can't understand these things. We are different.'

'I imagine that you are human beings, even though England and America respectively had the intense good fortune of seeing your birth.'

'We're human beings—and more than that, we're nineteenth century human beings. Love is not everything. It is a part of one—perhaps the lower part—an accessory to man's life, needful for the continuation of the species.'

'You use such difficult words, my dear.'

'There is something higher and nobler and purer than love—there is friendship. Ferdinand White is my friend. I have the amplest confidence in him. I am certain that no unclean thought has ever entered his head.'

She spoke quite heatedly, and as she flushed up, the old painter thought her astonishingly handsome. Then she added as an afterthought,—

'We despise passion. Passion is ugly; it is grotesque.'

The painter stroked his imperial and faintly smiled.

'My child, you must permit me to tell you that you are foolish. Passion is the most lovely thing in the world; without it we should not paint beautiful pictures. It is passion that makes a woman of a society lady; it is passion that makes a man even of—an art critic.'

'We do not want it,' she said. 'We worship Venus Urania. We are all spirit and soul.'

'You have been reading Plato; soon you will read Zola.'

He smiled again, and lit another cigarette.

'Do you disapprove of my going?' she asked after a little silence.

He paused and looked at her. Then he shrugged his shoulders.

'On the contrary, I approve. It is foolish, but that is no reason why you should not do it. After all, folly is the great attribute of man. No judge is as grave as an owl; no soldier fighting for his country flies as rapidly as the hare. You may be strong, but you are not so strong as a horse; you may be gluttonous, but you cannot eat like a boa-constrictor. But there is no beast that can be as foolish as man. And since one should always do what one can do best—be foolish. Strive for folly above all things. Let the height of your ambition be the pointed cap with the golden bells. So, *bon voyage!* I will come and see you off to-morrow.'

The painter arrived at the station with a box of sweets, which he handed to Valentia with a smile. He shook Ferdinand's hand warmly and muttered under his breath,—

'Silly fool! he's thinking of friendship, too!'

Then, as the train steamed out, he waved his hand and cried,—

'Be foolish! Be foolish!'

He walked slowly out of the station, and sat down at a café. He lit a cigarette, and, sipping his absinthe, said,—

'Imbeciles!'

III

They arrived at Amsterdam in the evening, and, after dinner, gathered together their belongings and crossed the Ij as the moon shone over the waters; then they got into the little steam tram and started for Monnickendam. They stood side by side on the platform of the carriage and watched the broad meadows bathed in moonlight, the formless shapes of the cattle lying on the grass, and the black outlines of the mills; they passed by a long, sleeping canal, and they stopped at little, silent villages. At last they entered the dead town, and the tram put them down at the hotel door.

Next morning, when she was half dressed, Valentia threw open the window of her room, and looked out into the garden.

Ferdinand was walking about, dressed as befitted the place and season—in flannels—with a huge white hat on his head. She could not help thinking him very handsome—and she took off the blue skirt she had intended to work in, and put on a dress of muslin all bespattered with coloured flowers, and she took in her hand a flat straw hat with red ribbons.

'You look like a Dresden shepherdess,' he said, as they met.

They had breakfast in the garden beneath the trees; and as she poured out his tea, she laughed, and with the American accent which he was beginning to think made English so harmonious, said,—

'I reckon this about takes the shine out of Paris.'

They had agreed to start work at once, losing no time, for they wanted to have a lot to show on their return to France, that their scheme might justify itself. Ferdinand wished to accompany Valentia on her search for the picturesque, but she would not let him; so, after breakfast, he sat himself down in the summer-house, and spread out all round him his nice white paper, lit his pipe, cut his quills, and proceeded to the evolution of a masterpiece. Valentia tied the red strings of her sun-bonnet under her chin, selected a sketchbook, and sallied forth.

At luncheon they met, and Valentia told of a little bit of canal, with an old windmill on one side of it, which she had decided to paint, while Ferdinand announced that he had settled

on the names of his *dramatis personæ*. In the afternoon they returned to their work, and at night, tired with the previous day's
travelling, went to bed soon after dinner.

So passed the second day; and the third day, and the fourth;
till the end of the week came, and they had worked diligently.
They were both of them rather surprised at the ease with which
they became accustomed to their life.

'How absurd all this fuss is,' said Valentia, 'that people make
about the differences of the sexes! I am sure it is only habit.'

'We have ourselves to prove that there is nothing in it,' he
replied. 'You know, it is an interesting experiment that we are
making.'

She had not looked at it in that light before.

'Perhaps it is. We may be the fore-runners of a new era.'

'The Edisons of a new communion!'

'I shall write and tell Monsieur Rollo all about it.'

In the course of the letter, she said,—

*'Sex is a morbid instinct. Out here, in the calmness of the canal
and the broad meadows, it never enters one's head. I do not think of
Ferdinand as a man—'*

She looked up at him as she wrote the words. He was reading a book and she saw him in profile, with the head bent down.
Through the leaves the sun lit up his face with a soft light that

was almost green, and it occurred to her that it would be interesting to paint him.

'I do not think of Ferdinand as a man; to me he is a companion. He has a wider experience than a woman, and he talks of different things. Otherwise I see no difference. On his part, the idea of my sex never occurs to him, and far from being annoyed as an ordinary woman might be, I am proud of it. It shows me that, when I chose a companion, I chose well. To him I am not a woman; I am a man.'

And she finished with a repetition of Ferdinand's remark,— 'We are the Edisons of a new communion!'

When Valentia began to paint her companion's portrait, they were naturally much more together. And they never grew tired of sitting in the pleasant garden under the trees, while she worked at her canvas and green shadows fell on the profile of Ferdinand White. They talked of many things. After a while they became less reserved about their private concerns. Valentia told Ferdinand about her home in Ohio, and about her people; and Ferdinand spoke of the country parsonage in which he had spent his childhood, and the public school, and lastly of Oxford and the strange, happy days when he had learnt to read Plato and Walter Pater. . . .

At last Valentia threw aside her brushes and leant back with a sigh.

'It is finished!'

Ferdinand rose and stretched himself, and went to look at his portrait. He stood before it for a while, and then he placed his hand on Valentia's shoulder.

'You are a genius, Miss Stewart.'

She looked up at him.

'Ah, Mr White, I was inspired by you. It is more your work than mine.'

IV

In the evening they went out for a stroll. They wandered through the silent street; in the darkness they lost the quaintness of the red brick houses, contrasting with the bright yellow of the paving, but it was even quieter than by day. The street was very broad, and it wound about from east to west and from west to east, and at last it took them to the tiny harbour. Two fishing smacks were basking on the water, moored to the side, and the Zuyder Zee was covered with the innumerable reflections of the stars. On one of the boats a man was sitting at the prow, fishing, and now and then, through the darkness, one saw the red glow of his pipe; by his side, huddled up on a sail, lay a sleeping boy. The other boat seemed deserted. Ferdinand and Valentia stood for a long time watching the fisher, and he was so still that they wondered whether he too were sleeping. They looked across the sea, and in the distance saw the dim lights of Marken, the island of fishers. They wandered on again through the street, and now the lights in the windows were extinguished one by one, and sleep came over the town; and the quietness was even greater than before. They walked on, and their footsteps made no sound. They felt themselves alone in the dead city, and they did not speak.

At length they came to a canal gliding towards the sea; they followed it inland, and here the darkness was equal to the silence. Great trees that had been planted when William of Orange was king in England threw their shade over the water, shutting out the stars. They wandered along on the soft earth, they could not hear themselves walk—and they did not speak.

They came to a bridge over the canal and stood on it, looking at the water and the trees above them, and the water and the trees below them—and they did not speak.

Then out of the darkness came another darkness, and gradually loomed forth the heaviness of a barge. Noiselessly it glided down the stream, very slowly; at the end of it a boy stood at the tiller, steering; and it passed beneath them and beyond, till it lost itself in the night, and again they were alone.

They stood side by side, leaning against the parapet, looking down at the water.... And from the water rose up Love, and Love fluttered down from the trees, and Love was borne along upon the night air. Ferdinand did not know what was happening to him; he felt Valentia by his side, and he drew closer to her, till her dress touched his legs and the silk of her sleeve rubbed against his arm. It was so dark that he could not see her face; he wondered of what she was thinking. She made a little movement and to him came a faint wave of the scent she wore. Presently two forms passed by on the bank and they saw a lover with his arm round a girl's waist, and then they too were hidden in the darkness. Ferdinand trembled as he spoke.

'Only Love is waking!'

'And we!' she said.

'And—you!'

He wondered why she said nothing. Did she understand? He put his hand on her arm.

'Valentia!'

He had never called her by her Christian name before. She turned her face towards him.

'What do you mean?'

'Oh, Valentia, I love you! I can't help it.'

A sob burst from her.

'Didn't you understand,' he said, 'all those hours that I sat for you while you painted, and these long nights in which we wandered by the water?'

'I thought you were my friend.'

'I thought so too. When I sat before you and watched you paint, and looked at your beautiful hair and your eyes, I thought I was your friend. And I looked at the lines of your body beneath your dress. And when it pleased me to carry your easel and walk with you, I thought it was friendship. Only to-night I know I am in love. Oh, Valentia, I am so glad!'

She could not keep back her tears. Her bosom heaved, and she wept.

'You are a woman,' he said. 'Did you not see?'

'I am so sorry,' she said, her voice all broken. 'I thought we were such good friends. I was so happy. And now you have spoilt it all.'

'Valentia, I love you.'

'I thought our friendship was so good and pure. And I felt so strong in it. It seemed to me so beautiful.'

'Did you think I was less a man than the fisherman you see walking beneath the trees at night?'

'It is all over now,' she sighed.

'What do you mean?'

'I can't stay here with you alone.'

'You're not going away?'

'Before, there was no harm in our being together at the ho-tel; but now—'

'Oh, Valentia, don't leave me. I can't—I can't live without you.'

She heard the unhappiness in his voice. She turned to him again and laid her two hands on his shoulders.

'Why can't you forget it all, and let us be good friends again? Forget that you are a man. A woman can remain with a man for ever, and always be content to walk and read and talk with him, and never think of anything else. Can you forget it, Ferdinand? You will make me so happy.'

He did not answer, and for a long time they stood on the bridge in silence. At last he sighed—a heartbroken sigh.

'Perhaps you're right. It may be better to pretend that we are friends. If you like, we will forget all this.'

Her heart was too full; she could not answer; but she held out her hands to him. He took them in his own, and, bending down, kissed them.

Then they walked home, side by side, without speaking.

V

Next morning Valentia received M. Rollo's answer to her letter. He apologised for his delay in answering.

'You are a philosopher,' he said—she could see the little snigger with which he had written the words—'You are a philosopher, and I was afraid lest my reply should disturb the course of your reflections on friendship. I confess that I did not entirely understand your letter, but I gathered that the sentiments were correct, and it gave me great pleasure to know that your experiment has had such excellent results. I gather that you have not yet discovered that there is more than a verbal connection between Friendship and Love.'

The reference is to the French equivalents of those states of mind.

'*But to speak seriously, dear child. You are young and beautiful now, but not so very many years shall pass before your lovely skin becomes coarse and muddy, and your teeth yellow, and the wrinkles appear about your mouth and eyes. You have not so very many years before you in which to collect sensations, and the recollection of one's loves is, perhaps, the greatest pleasure left to one's old age. To be virtuous, my dear, is admirable, but there are so many interpretations of virtue. For myself, I can say that I have never regretted the temptations to which I succumbed, but often the temptations I have resisted. Therefore, love, love, love! And remember that if love at sixty in a man is sometimes pathetic, in a woman at forty it is always ridiculous. Therefore, take your youth in both hands and say to yourself, "Life is short, but let me live before I die!"*'

She did not show the letter to Ferdinand.

Next day it rained. Valentia retired to a room at the top of the house and began to paint, but the incessant patter on the roof got on her nerves; the painting bored her, and she threw aside the brushes in disgust. She came downstairs and found Ferdinand in the dining-room, standing at the window looking at the rain. It came down in one continual steady pour, and the water ran off the raised brickwork of the middle of the street to the gutters by the side, running along in a swift and murky rivulet. The red brick of the opposite house looked cold and cheerless in the wet. . . . He did not turn or speak to her as she came in. She remarked that it did not look like leaving off. He made no answer. She drew a chair to the second window and tried to read, but she could not understand what she was reading. And she looked out at the pouring rain and the red brick house opposite. She wondered why he had not answered.

The innkeeper brought them their luncheon. Ferdinand took no notice of the preparations.

'Will you come to luncheon, Mr White?' she said to him. 'It is quite ready.'

'I beg your pardon,' he said gravely, as he took his seat.

He looked at her quickly, and then immediately dropping his eyes, began eating. She wished he would not look so sad; she was very sorry for him.

She made an observation and he appeared to rouse himself. He replied and they began talking, very calmly and coldly, as if they had not known one another five minutes. They talked of Art with the biggest of A's, and they compared Dutch painting with Italian; they spoke of Rembrandt and his life.

'Rembrandt had passion,' said Ferdinand, bitterly, 'and therefore he was unhappy. It is only the sexless, passionless creature, the block of ice, that can be happy in this world.'

25

She blushed and did not answer.

The afternoon Valentia spent in her room, pretending to write letters, and she wondered whether Ferdinand was wishing her downstairs.

At dinner they sought refuge in abstractions. They talked of dykes and windmills and cigars, the history of Holland and its constitution, the constitution of the United States and the edifying spectacle of the politics of that blessed country. They talked of political economy and pessimism and cattle rearing, the state of agriculture in England, the foreign policy of the day, Anarchism, the President of the French Republic. They would have talked of bi-metallism if they could. People hearing them would have thought them very learned and extraordinarily staid.

At last they separated, and as she undressed Valentia told herself that Ferdinand had kept his promise. Everything was just as it had been before, and the only change was that he used her Christian name. And she rather liked him to call her Valentia.

But next day Ferdinand did not seem able to command himself. When Valentia addressed him, he answered in mono-syllables, with eyes averted; but when she had her back turned, she felt that he was looking at her. After breakfast she went away painting haystacks, and was late for luncheon.

She apologised.

'It is of no consequence,' he said, keeping his eyes on the ground. And those were the only words he spoke to her during the remainder of the day. Once, when he was looking at her surreptitiously, and she suddenly turned round, their eyes met, and for a moment he gazed straight at her, then walked away. She wished he would not look so sad. As she was going to bed, she held out her hand to him to say good-night, and she added,—

'I don't want to make you unhappy, Mr White. I'm very sorry.'

'It's not your fault,' he said. 'You can't help it, if you're a stock and a stone.'

He went away without taking the proffered hand. Valentia cried that night.

In the morning she found a note outside her door:—

'Pardon me if I was rude, but I was not master of myself. I am going to Volendam; I hate Monnickendam.'

VI

Ferdinand arrived at Volendam. It was a fishing village, only three miles across country from Monnickendam, but the route, by steam tram and canal, was so circuitous, that, with luggage, it took one two hours to get from place to place. He had walked over there with Valentia, and it had almost tempted them to desert Monnickendam. Ferdinand took a room at the hotel and walked out, trying to distract himself. The village consisted of a couple of score of houses, built round a semi-circular dyke against the sea, and in the semi-circle lay the fleet of fishing boats. Men and women were sitting at their doors mending nets. He looked at the fishermen, great, sturdy fellows, with rough, weather-beaten faces, huge earrings dangling from their ears. He took note of their quaint costume—black stockings and breeches, the latter more baggy than a Turk's, and the crushed strawberry of their high jackets, cut close to the body. He remembered how he had looked at them with Valentia, and the group of boys and men that she had sketched. He remembered how they walked along, peeping into the houses, where everything was spick and span, as only a Dutch cottage can be, with old Delft plates hanging on the walls, and pots and pans of polished brass. And he looked over the sea to the island of Marken, with its masts crowded together, like a forest without leaf or branch. Coming to the end of the little town he saw the church of Monnickendam, the red steeple half-hidden by the trees. He wondered where Valentia was—what she was doing.

But he turned back resolutely, and, going to his room, opened his books and began reading. He rubbed his eyes and frowned, in order to fix his attention, but the book said nothing but Valentia. At last he threw it aside and took his Plato and his dictionary, commencing to translate a difficult passage, word for word. But whenever he looked up a word he could only see Valentia, and he could not make head or tail of the Greek. He threw it aside also, and set out walking. He walked as hard as he could—away from Monnickendam.

The second day was not quite so difficult, and he read till his mind was dazed, and then he wrote letters home and told them he was enjoying himself tremendously, and he walked till he felt his legs dropping off.

Next morning it occurred to him that Valentia might have written. Trembling with excitement, he watched the postman coming down the street—but he had no letter for Ferdinand. There would be no more post that day.

But the next day Ferdinand felt sure there would be a letter for him; the postman passed by the hotel door without stopping. Ferdinand thought he should go mad. All day he walked up and down his room, thinking only of Valentia. Why did she not write?

The night fell and he could see from his window the moon shining over the clump of trees about Monnickendam church—he could stand it no longer. He put on his hat and walked across country; the three miles were endless; the church and the trees seemed to grow no nearer, and at last, when he thought himself close, he found he had a bay to walk round, and it appeared further away than ever.

He came to the mouth of the canal along which he and Valentia had so often walked. He looked about, but he could see no one. His heart beat as he approached the little bridge, but Valentia was not there. Of course she would not come out alone. He ran to the hotel and asked for her. They told him she was not in. He walked through the town; not a soul was to be seen. He came to the church; he walked round, and then—right at the edge of the trees—he saw a figure sitting on a bench.

〜

She was dressed in the same flowered dress which she had worn when he likened her to a Dresden shepherdess; she was looking towards Volendam.

He went up to her silently. She sprang up with a little shriek. 'Ferdinand!'

'Oh, Valentia, I cannot help it. I could not remain away any longer. I could do nothing but think of you all day, all night. If you knew how I loved you! Oh, Valentia, have pity on me! I cannot be your friend. It's all nonsense about friendship; I hate it. I can only love you. I love you with all my heart and soul, Valentia.'

She was frightened.

'Oh! how can you stand there so coldly and watch my agony? Don't you see? How can you be so cold?'

'I am not cold, Ferdinand,' she said, trembling. 'Do you think I have been happy while you were away?'

'Valentia!'

'I thought of you, too, Ferdinand, all day, all night. And I longed for you to come back. I did not know till you went that—I loved you.'

'Oh, Valentia!'

He took her in his arms and pressed her passionately to him.

'No, for God's sake!'

She tore herself away. But again he took her in his arms, and this time he kissed her on the mouth. She tried to turn her face away.

'I shall kill myself, Ferdinand!'

'What do you mean?'

'In those long hours that I sat here looking towards you, I felt I loved you—I loved you as passionately as you said you loved me. But if you came back, and—anything happened—I swore that I would throw myself in the canal.'

He looked at her.

'I could not—live afterwards,' she said hoarsely. 'It would be too horrible. I should be—oh, I can't think of it!'

He took her in his arms again and kissed her.

'Have mercy on me!' she cried.

'You love me, Valentia.'

'Oh, it is nothing to you. Afterwards you will be just the same as before. Why cannot men love peacefully like women? I should be so happy to remain always as we are now, and never change. I tell you I shall kill myself.'

'I will do as you do, Valentia.'

'You?'

'If anything happens, Valentia,' he said gravely, 'we will go down to the canal together.'

She was horrified at the idea; but it fascinated her.

'I should like to die in your arms,' she said.

For the second time he bent down and took her hands and kissed them. Then she went alone into the silent church, and prayed.

VII

They went home. Ferdinand was so pleased to be at the hotel again, near her. His bed seemed so comfortable; he was
so happy, and he slept, dreaming of Valentia.

The following night they went for their walk, arm in arm;
and they came to the canal. From the bridge they looked at the
water. It was very dark; they could not hear it flow. No stars were
reflected in it, and the trees by its side made the depth seem endless. Valentia shuddered. Perhaps in a little while their bodies
would be lying deep down in the water. And they would be in
one another's arms, and they would never be separated. Oh,
what a price it was to pay! She looked tearfully at Ferdinand, but
he was looking down at the darkness beneath them, and he was
intensely grave.

And they wandered there by day and looked at the black reflection of the trees. And in the heat it seemed so cool and restful....

They abandoned their work. What did pictures and books matter now? They sauntered about the meadows, along shady roads; they watched the black and white cows sleepily browsing, sometimes coming to the water's edge to drink, and looking at themselves, amazed. They saw the huge-limbed milkmaids come along with their little stools and their pails, deftly tying the cow's hind legs that it might not kick. And the steaming milk frothed into the pails and was poured into huge barrels, and as each cow was freed, she shook herself a little and recommenced to browse.

And they loved their life as they had never loved it before.

One evening they went again to the canal and looked at the water, but they seemed to have lost their emotions before it. They were no longer afraid. Ferdinand sat on the parapet and Valentia leaned against him. He bent his head so that his face might touch her hair. She looked at him and smiled, and she almost lifted her lips. He kissed them.

'Do you love me, Ferdinand?'

He gave the answer without words.

Their faces were touching now, and he was holding her hands. They were both very happy.

'You know, Ferdinand,' she whispered, 'we are very foolish.'

'I don't care.'

'Monsieur Rollo said that folly was the chief attribute of man.'

'What did he say of love?'

'I forget.'

Then, after a pause, he whispered in her ear,—

'I love you!'

And she held up her lips to him again.

'After all,' she said, 'we're only human beings. We can't help it. I think—'

She hesitated; what she was going to say had something of the anti-climax in it.

'I think—it would be very silly if—if we threw ourselves in the horrid canal.'

'Valentia, do you mean—?'

She smiled charmingly as she answered,—

'What you will, Ferdinand.'

Again he took both her hands, and, bending down, kissed them. . . . But this time she lifted him up to her and kissed him on the lips.

VIII

One night after dinner I told this story to my aunt.
'But why on earth didn't they get married?' she asked,
when I had finished.

'Good Heavens!' I cried. 'It never occurred to me.'

'Well, I think they ought,' she said.

'Oh, I have no doubt they did. I expect they got on their
bikes and rode off to the Consulate at Amsterdam there and
then. I'm sure it would have been his first thought.'

'Of course, some girls are very queer,' said my aunt.

THE PUNCTILIOUSNESS
OF DON SEBASTIAN

I

Xiormonez is the most inaccessible place in Spain. Only one train arrives there in the course of the day, and that arrives at two o'clock in the morning; only one train leaves it, and that starts an hour before sunrise. No one has ever been able to discover what happens to the railway officials during the intermediate one-and-twenty hours. A German painter I met there, who had come by the only train, and had been endeavouring for a fortnight to get up in time to go away, told me that he had frequently gone to the station in order to clear up the mystery, but had never been able to do so; yet, from his inquiries, he was inclined to suspect—that was as far as he would commit himself, being a cautious man—that they spent the time in eating garlic and smoking execrable cigarettes. The guide-books tell you that Xiormonez possesses the eyebrows of Joseph of Arimathea, a cathedral of the greatest quaintness, and battlements untouched since their erection in the fourteenth century. And they strongly advise you to visit it, but recommend you before doing so to add Keating's insect powder to your other toilet necessaries.

I was travelling to Madrid in an express train which had been rushing along at the pace of sixteen miles an hour, when suddenly it stopped. I leant out of the window, asking where we were.

'Xiormonez!' answered the guard.

'I thought we did not stop at Xiormonez.'

'We do not stop at Xiormonez,' he replied impassively.

'But we are stopping now!'

'That may be; but we are going on again.'

I had already learnt that it was folly to argue with a Spanish guard, and, drawing back my head, I sat down. But, looking at my watch, I saw that it was only ten. I should never again have a chance of inspecting the eyebrows of Joseph of Arimathea unless I chartered a special train, so, seizing the opportunity and my bag, I jumped out.

The only porter told me that everyone in Xiormonez was asleep at that hour, and recommended me to spend the night in the waiting-room, but I bribed him heavily; I offered him two pesetas, which is nearly fifteenpence, and, leaving the train to its own devices, he shouldered my bag and started off.

Along a stony road we walked into the dark night, the wind blowing cold and bitter, and the clouds chasing one another across the sky. In front, I could see nothing but the porter hurrying along, bent down under the weight of my bag, and the wind blew icily. I buttoned up my coat. And then I regretted the warmth of the carriage, the comfort of my corner and my rug; I wished I had peacefully continued my journey to Madrid—I was on the verge of turning back as I heard the whistling of the train. I hesitated, but the porter hurried on, and fearing to lose him in the night, I sprang forwards. Then the puffing of the engine, and on the smoke the bright reflection of the furnace, and the train steamed away; like Abd-er-Rahman, I felt that I had flung my scabbard into the flames.

Still the porter hurried on, bent down under the weight of my bag, and I saw no light in front of me to announce the approach to a town. On each side, bordering the road, were trees, and beyond them darkness. And great black clouds hastened after one another across the heavens. Then, as we walked along, we came to a rough stone cross, and lying on the steps before it was a woman with uplifted hands. And the wind blew bitter and keen, freezing the marrow of one's bones. What prayers had she to offer that she must kneel there alone in the night? We passed another cross standing up with its outstretched arms like a soul in pain. At last a heavier night rose before me, and presently I saw a great stone arch. Passing beneath it, I found myself immediately in the town.

The street was tortuous and narrow, paved with rough cobbles; and it rose steeply, so that the porter bent lower beneath his burden, panting. With the bag on his shoulders he looked like some hunchbacked gnome, a creature of nightmare. On either side rose tall houses, lying crooked and irregular, leaning towards one another at the top, so that one could not see the clouds, and their windows were great, black apertures like giant mouths. There was not a light, not a soul, not a sound—except that of my own feet and the heavy panting of the porter. We wound through the streets, round corners, through low arches, a long way up the steep cobbles, and suddenly down broken steps. They hurt my feet, and I stumbled and almost fell, but the hunchback walked along nimbly, hurrying ever. Then we came into an open space, and the wind caught us again, and blew through our clothes, so that I shrank up, shivering. And never a soul did we see as we walked on; it might have been a city of the dead. Then past a tall church: I saw a carved porch, and from the side grim devils grinning down upon me; the porter dived through an arch, and I groped my way along a narrow passage. At length he stopped, and with a sigh threw down the bag. He beat with his fists against an iron door, making the metal ring. A window above was thrown open, and a voice cried out. The porter answered; there was a clattering down the stairs, an unlocking, and the door was timidly held open, so that I saw a woman, with the light of her candle throwing a strange yellow glare on her face.

And so I arrived at the hotel of Xiormonez.

II

My night was troubled by the ghostly crying of the watch-man: 'Protect us, Mary, Queen of Heaven; protect us, Mary!' Every hour it rang out stridently as soon as the heavy bells of the cathedral had ceased their clanging, and I thought of the woman kneeling at the cross, and wondered if her soul had found peace.

In the morning I threw open the windows and the sun came dancing in, flooding the room with gold. In front of me the great wall of the cathedral stood grim and grey, and the gargoyles looked savagely across the square.... The cathedral is admirable; when you enter you find yourself at once in darkness, and the air is heavy with incense; but, as your eyes become accustomed to the gloom, you see the black forms of penitents kneeling by pillars, looking towards an altar, and by the light of the painted windows a reredos, with the gaunt saints of an early painter, and aureoles shining dimly.

But the gem of the Cathedral of Xiormonez is the Chapel of the Duke de Losas, containing, as it does, the alabaster monument of Don Sebastian Emanuel de Mantona, Duque de Losas, and of the very illustrious Señora Doña Sodina de Berruguete, his wife. Like everything else in Spain, the chapel is kept locked up, and the guide-book tells you to apply to the porter at the palace of the present duke. I sent a little boy to fetch that worthy, who presently came back, announcing that the porter and his wife had gone into the country for the day, but that the duke was coming in person.

And immediately I saw walking towards me a little, dark man, wrapped up in a big capa, with the red and blue velvet of the lining flung gaudily over his shoulder. He bowed courteously as he approached, and I perceived that on the crown his hair was somewhat more than thin. I hesitated a little, rather awkwardly, for the guide-book said that the porter exacted a fee of one peseta for opening the chapel—one could scarcely offer sevenpence-halfpenny to a duke. But he quickly put an end to all doubt, for, as he unlocked the door, he turned to me and said,—

'The fee is one franc.'

As I gave it him he put it in his pocket and gravely handed me a little printed receipt. Baedeker had obligingly informed me that the Duchy of Losas was shorn of its splendour, but I had not understood that the present representative added to his income by exhibiting the bones of his ancestors at a franc a head. . . .

We entered, and the duke pointed out the groining of the roof and the tracery of the windows.

'This chapel contains some of the finest Gothic in Spain,' he said.

When he considered that I had sufficiently admired the architecture, he turned to the pictures, and, with the fluency of a professional guide, gave me their subjects and the names of the artists.

'Now we come to the tombs of Don Sebastian, the first Duke of Losas, and his spouse, Doña Sodina—not, however, the first duchess.'

The monument stood in the middle of the chapel, covered with a great pall of red velvet, so that no economical tourist should see it through the bars of the gate and thus save his peseta. The duke removed the covering and watched me silently, a slight smile trembling below his little, black moustache.

The duke and his wife, who was not his duchess, lay side by side on a bed of carved alabaster; at the corners were four twisted pillars, covered with little leaves and flowers, and between them bas-reliefs representing Love, and Youth, and Strength, and Pleasure, as if, even in the midst of death, death must be forgotten. Don Sebastian was in full armour. His helmet was admirably carved with a representation of the battle between the Centaurs and the Lapithæ; on the right arm-piece were portrayed the adventures of Venus and Mars, on the left the emotions of Vulcan; but on the breast-plate was an elaborate Crucifixion, with soldiers and women and apostles. The visor was raised, and showed a stern, heavy face, with prominent cheek bones, sensual lips and a massive chin.

'It is very fine,' I remarked, thinking the duke expected some remark.

'People have thought so for three hundred years,' he replied gravely.

He pointed out to me the hands of Don Sebastian.

'The guide-books have said that they are the finest hands in Spain. Tourists especially admire the tendons and veins, which, as you perceive, stand out as in no human hand would be possible. They say it is the summit of art.'

And he took me to the other side of the monument, that I might look at Doña Sodina.

'They say she was the most beautiful woman of her day,' he said, 'but in that case the Castilian lady is the only thing in Spain which has not degenerated.'

She was, indeed, not beautiful: her face was fat and broad, like her husband's; a short, ungraceful nose, and a little, nobbly chin; a thick neck, set dumpily on her marble shoulders. One could not but hope that the artist had done her an injustice.

The Duke of Losas made me observe the dog which was lying at her feet.

'It is a symbol of fidelity,' he said.

'The guide-book told me she was chaste and faithful.'

'If she had been,' he replied, smiling, 'Don Sebastian would perhaps never have become Duque de Losas.'

'Really!'

'It is an old history which I discovered one day among some family papers.'

I pricked up my ears, and discreetly began to question him.

'Are you interested in old manuscripts?' said the duke. 'Come with me and I will show you what I have.'

With a flourish of the hand he waved me out of the chapel, and, having carefully locked the doors, accompanied me to his palace. He took me into a Gothic chamber, furnished with worn French furniture, the walls covered with cheap paper. Offering me a cigarette, he opened a drawer and produced a faded manuscript.

'This is the document in question,' he said. 'Those crooked and fantastic characters are terrible. I often wonder if the writers were able to read them.'

'You are fortunate to be the possessor of such things,' I remarked.

He shrugged his shoulders.

'What good are they? I would sooner have fifty pesetas than this musty parchment.'

An offer! I quickly reckoned it out into English money. He would doubtless have taken less, but I felt a certain delicacy in bargaining with a duke over his family secrets. . . .

'Do you mean it? May I—er—'

He sprang towards me.

'Take it, my dear sir, take it. Shall I give you a receipt?'

And so, for thirty-one shillings and threepence, I obtained the only authentic account of how the frailty of the illustrious Señora Doña Sodina was indirectly the means of raising her husband to the highest dignities in Spain.

III

Don Sebastian and his wife had lived together for fifteen years, with the entirest happiness to themselves and the greatest admiration of their neighbours. People said that such an example of conjugal felicity was not often seen in those degenerate days, for even then they prated of the golden age of their grandfathers, lamenting their own decadence. . . . As behoved good Castilians, burdened with such a line of noble ancestors, the fortunate couple conducted themselves with all imaginable gravity. No strange eye was permitted to witness a caress between the lord and his lady, or to hear an expression of endearment; but everyone could see the devotion of Don Sebastian, the look of adoration which filled his eyes when he gazed upon his wife. And people said that Doña Sodina was worthy of all his affection. They said that her virtue was only matched by her piety, and her piety was patent to the whole world, for every day she went to the cathedral at Xiormonez and remained long immersed in her devotions. Her charity was exemplary, and no beggar ever applied to her in vain.

But even if Don Sebastian and his wife had not possessed these conjugal virtues, they would have been in Xiormonez persons of note, since not only did they belong to an old and respected family, which was rich as well, but the gentleman's brother was archbishop of the See, who, when he graced the cathedral city with his presence, paid the greatest attention to Don Sebastian and Doña Sodina. Everyone said that the Archbishop Pablo would shortly become a cardinal, for he was a great favourite with the king, and with the latter His Holiness the Pope was then on terms of quite unusual friendship.

And in those days, when the priesthood was more noticeable for its gallantry than for its good works, it was refreshing to find so high-placed a dignitary of the Church a pattern of Christian virtues, who, notwithstanding his gorgeous habit of life, his retinue, his palaces, recalled, by his freedom from at least two of the seven deadly sins, the simplicity of the apostles, which the common people have often supposed the perfect state of the minister of God.

Don Sebastian had been affianced to Doña Sodina when he was a boy of ten, and before she could properly pronounce the viperish sibilants of her native tongue. When the lady attained her sixteenth year, the pair were solemnly espoused, and the young priest Pablo, the bridegroom's brother, assisted at the ceremony. In these days the union would have been instanced as a triumphant example of the success of the *mariage de convenance*, but at that time such arrangements were so usual that it never occurred to anyone to argue for or against them. Yet it was not customary for a young man of two-and-twenty to fall madly in love with the bride whom he saw for the first time a day or two before his marriage, and it was still less customary for the bride to give back an equal affection. For fifteen years the couple lived in harmony and contentment, with nothing to trouble the even tenor of their lives; and if there was a cloud in their sky, it was that a kindly Providence had vouchsafed no fruit to the union, notwithstanding the prayers and candles which Doña Sodina was known to have offered at the shrine of more than one saint in Spain who had made that kind of miracle particularly his own.

But even felicitous marriages cannot last for ever, since if the love does not die the lovers do. And so it came to pass that Doña Sodina, having eaten excessively of pickled shrimps, which the abbess of a highly respected convent had assured her were of great efficacy in the begetting of children, took a fever of the stomach, as the chronicle inelegantly puts it, and after a week of suffering was called to the other world, from which, as from the pickled shrimps, she had always expected much. There let us hope her virtues have been rewarded, and she rests in peace and happiness.

IV

When Don Sebastian walked from the cathedral to his house after the burial of his wife, no one saw a trace of emotion on his face, and it was with his wonted grave courtesy that he bowed to a friend as he passed him. Sternly and briefly, as usual, he gave orders that no one should disturb him, and went to the room of Doña Sodina; he knelt on the praying-stool which Doña Sodina had daily used for so many years, and he fixed his eyes on the crucifix hanging on the wall above it. The day passed, and the night passed, and Don Sebastian never moved—no thought or emotion entered him; being alive, he was like the dead; he was like the dead that linger on the outer limits of hell, with never a hope for the future, dull with the despair that shall last for ever and ever and ever. But when the woman who had nursed him in his childhood lovingly disobeyed his order and entered to give him food, she saw no tear in his eye, no sign of weeping.

'You are right!' he said, painfully rising from his knees. 'Give me to eat.'

Listlessly taking the food, he sank into a chair and looked at the bed on which had lately rested the corpse of Doña Sodina; but a kindly nature relieved his unhappiness, and he fell into a weary sleep.

When he awoke, the night was far advanced; the house, the town were filled with silence; all round him was darkness, and the ivory crucifix shone dimly, dimly. Outside the door a page was sleeping; he woke him and bade him bring light. . . . In his sorrow, Don Sebastian began to look at the things his wife had loved; he fingered her rosary, and turned over the pages of the half-dozen pious books which formed her library; he looked at the jewels which he had seen glittering on her bosom; the brocades, the rich silks, the cloths of gold and silver that she had delighted to wear. And at last he came across an old breviary which he thought she had lost—how glad she would have been to find it, she had so often regretted it! The pages were musty with their long concealment, and only faintly could be detected the scent which Doña Sodina used yearly to make and strew about her things. Turning over the pages listlessly, he saw some crabbed writing; he took it to the light—'*To-night, my beloved, I come.*' And the handwriting was that of Pablo, Archbishop of

Xiormonez. Don Sebastian looked at it long. Why should his brother write such words in the breviary of Doña Sodina? He turned the pages and the handwriting of his wife met his eye and the words were the same—'*To-night, my beloved, I come*'—as if they were such delight to her that she must write them herself. The breviary dropped from Don Sebastian's hand.

The taper, flickering in the draught, threw glaring lights on Don Sebastian's face, but it showed no change in it. He sat looking at the fallen breviary, and, in his mind, at the love which was dead. At last he passed his hand over his forehead.

'And yet,' he whispered, 'I loved thee well!'

But as the day came he picked up the breviary and locked it in a casket; he knelt again at the praying-stool and, lifting his hands to the crucifix, prayed silently. Then he locked the door of Doña Sodina's room, and it was a year before he entered it again.

That day the Archbishop Pablo came to his brother to offer consolation for his loss, and Don Sebastian at the parting kissed him on either cheek.

V

The people of Xiormonez said that Don Sebastian was heart-broken, for from the date of his wife's interment he was not seen in the streets by day. A few, returning home from some riot, had met him wandering in the dead of the night, but he passed them silently by. But he sent his servants to Toledo and Burgos, to Salamanca, Cordova, even to Paris and Rome; and from all these places they brought him books—and day after day he studied in them, till the common folk asked if he had turned magician.

So passed eleven months, and nearly twelve, till it wanted but five days to the anniversary of the death of Doña Sodina. Then Don Sebastian wrote to his brother the letter which for months he had turned over in his mind,—

W. Somerset Maugham

'*Seeing the instability of all human things, and the uncertain length of our exile upon earth, I have considered that it is evil for brothers to remain so separate. Therefore I implore you—who are my only relative in this world, and heir to all my goods and estates—to visit me quickly, for I have a presentiment that death is not far off, and I would see you before we are parted by the immense sea.*'

The archbishop was thinking that he must shortly pay a visit to his cathedral city, and, as his brother had desired, came to Xiormonez immediately. On the anniversary of Doña Sodina's interment, Don Sebastian entertained Archbishop Pablo to supper.

'My brother,' said he, to his guest, 'I have lately received from Cordova a wine which I desire you to taste. It is very highly prized in Africa, whence I am told it comes, and it is made with curious art and labour.'

Glass cups were brought, and the wine poured in. The archbishop was a connoisseur, and held it between the light and himself, admiring the sparkling clearness, and then inhaled the odour.

'It is nectar,' he said.

At last he sipped it.

'The flavour is very strange.'

He drank deeply. Don Sebastian looked at him and smiled

64

as his brother put down the empty glass. But when he was himself about to drink, the cup fell between his hands and the steward's, breaking into a hundred fragments, and the wine spilt on the floor.

'Fool!' cried Don Sebastian, and in his anger struck the servant.

But being a man of peace, the archbishop interposed.

'Do not be angry with him; it was an accident. There is more wine in the flagon.'

'No, I will not drink it,' said Don Sebastian, wrathfully. 'I will drink no more to-night.'

The archbishop shrugged his shoulders.

When they were alone, Don Sebastian made a strange request.

'My brother, it is a year to-day that Sodina was buried, and I have not entered her room since then. But now I have a desire to see it. Will you come with me?'

The archbishop consented, and together they crossed the long corridor that led to Doña Sodina's apartment, preceded by a boy with lights.

Don Sebastian unlocked the door, and, taking the taper from the page's hand, entered. The archbishop followed. The air was chill and musty, and even now an odour of recent death seemed to pervade the room.

Don Sebastian went to a casket, and from it took a breviary. He saw his brother start as his eye fell on it. He turned over the leaves till he came to a page on which was the archbishop's hand-writing, and handed it to him.

'Oh God!' exclaimed the priest, and looked quickly at the door. Don Sebastian was standing in front of it. He opened his mouth to cry out, but Don Sebastian interrupted him.

'Do not be afraid! I will not touch you.'

For a while they looked at one another silently; one pale, sweating with terror, the other calm and grave as usual. At last Don Sebastian spoke, hoarsely.

'Did she—did she love you?'

'Oh, my brother, forgive her. It was long ago—and she repented bitterly. And I—I!'

'I have forgiven you.'

The words were said so strangely that the archbishop shuddered. What did he mean?

Don Sebastian smiled.

'You have no cause for anxiety. From now it is finished. I will forget.' And, opening the door, he helped his brother across the threshold. The archbishop's hand was clammy as a hand of death.

When Don Sebastian bade his brother good-night, he kissed him on either cheek.

VI

The priest returned to his palace, and when he was in bed his secretary prepared to read to him, as was his wont, but the archbishop sent him away, desiring to be alone. He tried to think; but the wine he had drunk was heavy upon him, and he fell asleep. But presently he awoke, feeling thirsty; he drank some water. . . . Then he became strangely wide-awake, a feeling of uneasiness came over him as of some threatening presence behind him, and again he felt the thirst. He stretched out his hand for the flagon, but now there was a mist before his eyes and he could not see, his hand trembled so that he spilled the water. And the uneasiness was magnified till it became a terror, and the thirst was horrible. He opened his mouth to call out, but his throat was dry, so that no sound came. He tried to rise from his bed, but his limbs were heavy and he could not move. He breathed quicker and quicker, and his skin was extraordinarily dry. The terror became an agony; it was unbearable. He wanted to bury his face in the pillows to hide it from him; he felt the hair on his head hard and dry, and it stood on end! He called to God for help, but no sound came from his mouth. Then the terror took shape and form, and he knew that behind him was standing Doña Sodina, and she was looking at him with terrible, reproachful eyes. And a second Doña Sodina came and stood at the end of the bed, and another came by her side, and the room was filled with them. And his thirst was horrible; he tried to moisten his mouth with spittle, but the source of it was dry. Cramps seized his limbs, so that he writhed with pain. Presently a red glow fell upon the room and it became hot and hotter, till he gasped for breath; it blinded him, but he could not close his eyes. And he knew it was the glow of hell-fire, for in his ears rang the groans of souls in torment, and among the voices he recognised that of Doña Sodina, and then—then he heard his own voice. And, in the livid heat, he saw himself in his episcopal robes, lying on the ground, chained to Doña Sodina, hand and foot. And he knew that as long as heaven and earth should last, the torment of hell would continue.

When the priests came in to their master in the morning, they found him lying dead, with his eyes wide open, staring with a ghastly brilliancy into the unknown. Then there was weeping and lamentation, and from house to house the people told one another that the archbishop had died in his sleep. The bells were set tolling, and as Don Sebastian, in his solitude, heard them, referring to the chief ingredient of that strange wine from Cordova, he permitted himself the only jest of his life.

'It was *Belladonna* that sent his body to the worms; and it was *Belladonna* that sent his soul to hell.'

VII

The chronicle does not state whether the thought of his brother's heritage had ever entered Don Sebastian's head; but the fact remains that he was sole heir, and the archbishop had gathered the loaves and fishes to such purpose during his life that his death made Don Sebastian one of the wealthiest men in Spain. The simplest actions in this world, oh Martin Tupper! have often the most unforeseen results.

Now, Don Sebastian had always been ambitious, and his changed circumstances made him realise more clearly than ever that his merit was worthy of a brilliant arena. The times were propitious, for the old king had just died, and the new one had sent away the army of priests and monks which had turned every day into a Sunday; people said that God Almighty had had His day, and that the heathen deities had come to rule in His stead. From all corners of Spain gallants were coming to enjoy the sunshine, and everyone who could make a compliment or a graceful bow was sure of a welcome.

So Don Sebastian prepared to go to Madrid. But before leaving his native town he thought well to appease a possibly vengeful Providence by erecting in the cathedral a chapel in honour of his patron saint; not that he thought the saints would trouble themselves about the death of his brother, even though the causes of it were not entirely natural, but Don Sebastian remembered that Pablo was an archbishop, and the fact caused him a certain anxiety. He called together architects and sculptors, and ordered them to erect an edifice befitting his dignity; and being a careful man, as all Spaniards are, thought he would serve himself as well as the saint, and bade the sculptors make an image of Doña Sodina and an image of himself, in order that he might use the chapel also as a burial-place.

To pay for this, Don Sebastian left the revenue of several of his brother's farms, and then, with a peaceful conscience, set out for the capital.

At Madrid he laid himself out to gain the favour of his sovereign, and by dint of unceasing flattery soon received much of the king's attention; and presently Philip deigned to ask his advice on petty matters. And since Don Sebastian took care to advise as he saw the king desired, the latter concluded that the courtier was a man of stamina and ability, and began to consult him on matters of state. Don Sebastian opined that the pleasure of the prince must always come before the welfare of the nation, and the king was so impressed with his sagacity that one day he asked his opinion on a question of precedence—to the indignation of the most famous councillors in the land.

But the haughty soul of Don Sebastian chafed because he was only one among many favourites. The court was full of flatterers as assiduous and as obsequious as himself; his proud Castilian blood could brook no companions. . . . But one day, as he was moodily waiting in the royal antechamber, thinking of these things, it occurred to him that a certain profession had always been in great honour among princes, and he remembered that he had a cousin of eighteen, who was being educated in a convent near Xiormonez. She was beautiful. With buoyant heart he went to his house and told his steward to fetch her from the convent at once. Within a fortnight she was at Madrid. . . . Mercia was presented to the queen in the presence of Philip, and Don Sebastian noticed that the royal eye lighted up as he gazed on the bashful maiden. Then all the proud Castilian had to do was to shut his eyes and allow the king to make his own opportunities. Within a week Mercia was created maid of honour to the queen, and Don Sebastian was seized with an indisposition which confined him to his room.

The king paid his court royally, which is, boldly; and Doña Mercia had received in the convent too religious an education not to know that it was her duty to grant the king whatever it graciously pleased him to ask. . . .

When Don Sebastian recovered from his illness, he found the world at his feet, for everyone was talking of the king's new mistress, and it was taken as a matter of course that her cousin and guardian should take a prominent part in the affairs of the country. But Don Sebastian was furious! He went to the king and bitterly reproached him for thus dishonouring him. . . . Philip was a humane and generous-minded man, and understood that with a certain temperament it might be annoying to have one's ward philander with a king, so he did his best to console the courtier. He called him his friend and brother; he told him he would always love him, but Don Sebastian would not be consoled. And nothing would comfort him except to be made High Admiral of the Fleet. Philip was charmed to settle the matter so simply, and as he delighted in generosity when to be generous cost him nothing, he also created Don Sebastian Duke of Losas, and gave him, into the bargain, the hand of the richest heiress in Spain.

And that is the end of the story of the punctiliousness of Don Sebastian. With his second wife he lived many years, beloved of his sovereign, courted by the world, honoured by all, till he was visited by the Destroyer of Delights and the Leveller of the Grandeur of this World. . . .

VIII

Towards evening, the Duke of Losas passed my hotel, and, seeing me at the door, asked if I had read the manuscript.

'I thought it interesting,' I said, a little coldly, for, of course, I knew no Englishman would have acted like Don Sebastian.

He shrugged his shoulders.

'It is not half so interesting as a good dinner.'

At these words I felt bound to offer him such hospitality as the hotel afforded. I found him a very agreeable messmate. He told me the further history of his family, which nearly became extinct at the end of the last century, since the only son of the seventh duke had, unfortunately, not been born of any duchess. But Ferdinand, who was then King of Spain, was unwilling that an ancient family should die out, and was, at the same time, sorely in want of money; so the titles and honours of the house were continued to the son of the seventh duke, and King Ferdinand built himself another palace.

'But now,' said my guest, mournfully shaking his head, 'it is finished. My palace and a few acres of barren rock are all that remain to me of the lands of my ancestors, and I am the last of the line.'

But I bade him not despair. He was a bachelor and a duke, and not yet forty. I advised him to go to the United States before they put a duty on foreign noblemen; this was before the war; and I recommended him to take Maida Vale and Manchester on his way. Personally, I gave him a letter of introduction to an heiress of my acquaintance at Hampstead; for even in these days it is not so bad a thing to be Duchess of Losas, and the present duke has no brother.

WHAT IS ART FICTION?

The intersection of art and life. Painting with words. Portmay Press brings contemporary and classic works of art fiction to a wide readership.

OTHER TITLES OF INTEREST FROM PORTMAY PRESS

Marriage of the Smila-Hoffmans
Maryann D'Agincourt

False Dawn
Edith Wharton

Art Fiction: Stories
Edited by Genevieve Sheets

Art Fiction Stories II
Edited by Ellen Francese

A Landscape Painter
Henry James